The FIRST HIPPO on the MOON

Illustrated by the artistic genius

Tony Ross

BASED ON A TRUE STORY

HarperCollins *Children's Books*

For Zachary and Elijah
D.W.
To Ben and Kate, my newest friends
T.R.

This is the tale of **two hippos**. Two hippos with **one dream**.

To be the very **First Hippo** on the **Moon**.

One enormously **rich** hippo – Hercules Waldorf-Franklin III –
paid for a **gigantic** Hippo Space Centre to be built to blast him there.

HERCULES
First Hippo
on the Moon

Sheila didn't. Yes the other hippopotamus's name was Sheila. One morning she announced...

"But, Sheila..." said her giraffe friend. "You don't have a space rocket."

"Then we'll make one, Keith," Sheila replied.

Yes the giraffe's name was Keith.

"Us hippos like to Dream Big!"

Sheila's friends got to work building *her a* **rocket.**

"Quick as you can!"

"Well you could **help** me, **dear!**"

Tina the elephant brought back the **biggest tree trunk** she could find.

Joyce the gorilla
fetched the
longest
vine.

And Derek the ostrich was given
the task of gathering the pongiest
mountain of rhinoceros
dung.

After many days and nights the
animals finally unveiled
their space rocket...

All they needed to do now was ignite the rhino dung and **blast** Sheila into space.

But before Sheila could say 'off' it started raining.

It rained. And rained. And rained. It was rainy season.
It didn't stop raining for five long months.

The moment the rain stopped Sheila began her countdown **again**.

"Three! Two! One! Blast off!"

The hippo-po-rocket **shot up** into the sky!

Zooooooooooooom

The hippopotamus watched as the **earth**
became smaller **and** smaller
and the **moon** became

bigger and
bigger.

But in
deep space
disaster
struck...

Sheila was so busy munching on her shrub sandwiches that she didn't spot what was **hurtling** towards her.

A giant asteroid.

Boom!

The hippo-po-rocket smashed into hundreds of pieces, sending the shocked hippopotamus spinning wildly through space. She tumbled towards the moon.

To her **astonishment** Sheila had landed on top of the other hippopotamus, just as he was taking his very **first hippo-po-step** on the moon's surface.

With a tear in her eye, Sheila trudged off to the hippo-po-rocket.
Her Big Dream had been **crushed**.

Seconds later Sheila realised that she **didn't** have
a **clue** how the hippo-po-rocket worked.

Roarrrrrr!

Entering the earth's atmosphere the hippo-po-rocket soon began burning up.
Within moments the hippopotamus's **bottom**
was **blazing** like the **sun.**

Sheila **hit** the earth with a giant **wallop!**

She lay motionless on the ground,
her bountiful behind **sizzling** like a sausage.

But she **wouldn't** wake up. This was the **saddest** day the jungle had **ever** seen.

Then out of the silence came **a sound**.

ppppp...ppppp...fffffffftttttt!

The distinctive sound of a **bottom burp**. All the animals stared at each other.
Who would dream of letting **one go** at such a sad time?

Now Sheila was **famous** all over the world as
the very First Hippopotamus on the Moon.

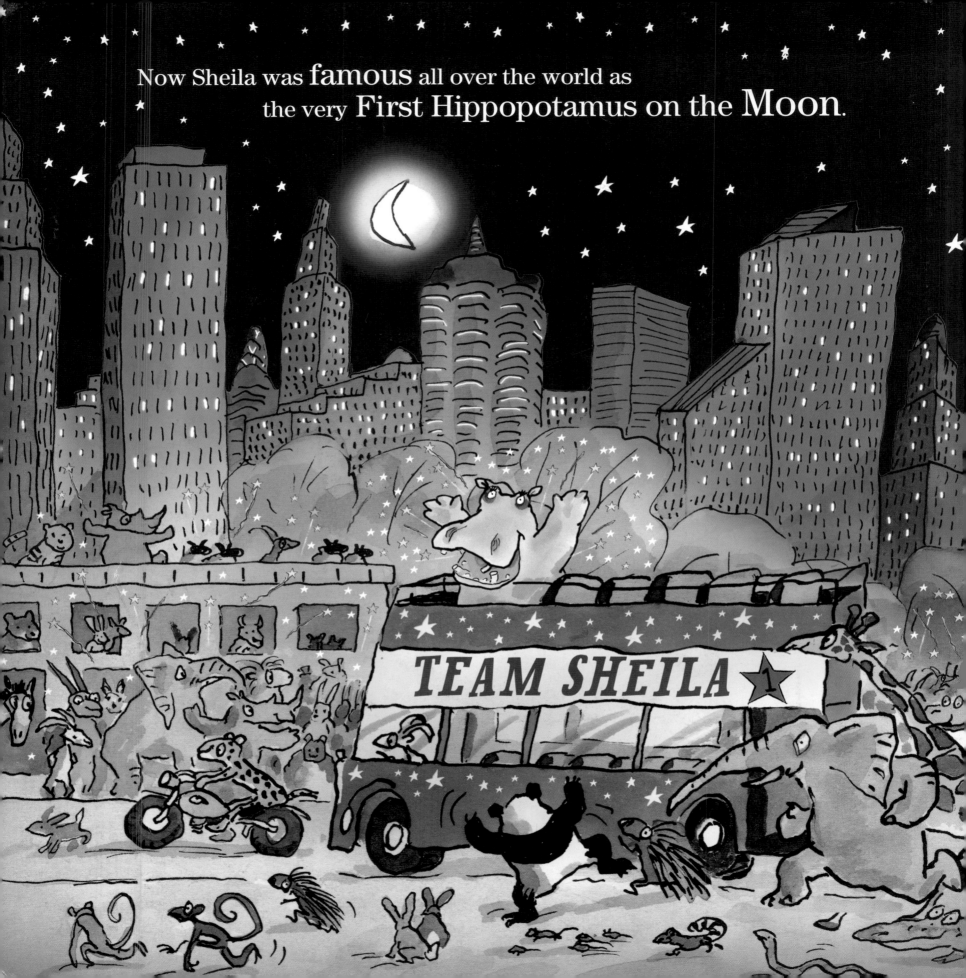

She never mentioned the other hippopotamus who got there first.

So whatever you do, please don't tell anyone.

First published in hardback by
HarperCollins Children's Books in 2014
First published in paperback in 2015

3 5 7 9 10 8 6 4 2

ISBN: 978-0-00-812186-0

HarperCollins Children's Books is a division of HarperCollins Publishers Ltd.

Text © David Walliams 2014
Illustrations © Tony Ross 2014
Cover lettering of author's name © Quentin Blake 2010

Printed and bound in Italy

David Walliams

PRESENTS...